Masai and I

and I

by **Virginia Kroll**

illustrations by **Nancy Carpenter**

Hamish Hamilton • London

HAMISH HAMILTON LTD

Published by the Penguin Group
27 Wrights Lane, London W8 5TZ, England
Penguin Books USA Inc, 375 Hudson Street, New York, New York 10014, U.S.A.
Penguin Books Australia Ltd, Ringwood, Victoria, Australia.
Penguin Books Canada Ltd, 10 Alcorn Avenue, Toronto, Ontario, Canada M4V 3B2
Penguin Books (NZ) Ltd, 182-190 Wairau Road, Auckland 10, New Zealand.

Penguin Books Ltd, Registered Offices: Harmondsworth, Middlesex, England.

First Published in Great Britain 1993 by Hamish Hamilton Ltd

Text copyright © 1992 by Virginia Kroll
Illustrations copyright © 1992 by Nancy Carpenter
Published by arrangement with Four Winds Press, Macmillan Publishing Company, USA
10 9 8 7 6 5 4 3 2 1

The moral right of the author (and artist) has been asserted

British Library Cataloguing in Publication Data
CIP data for this book is available from the British Library

ISBN 0-241-13311-4

Printed and bound in Hong Kong by Imago Publishing Ltd.

For my granddaughter, Olivia Hazel DeAnthony

—V.K.

To Jennie, for getting me started

—N.C.

That day at school, we learned about East Africa and a tall, proud people called the Masai. I feel the tingle of kinship flowing through my veins.

I walk home to our block of flats.
I've met Mrs Stroud across the passage and
the Johnson family in number 4, but that's all.
If I were Masai, I would have no neighbours
who were strangers living in flats up and down
the corridors. Our huts would sit in a circle
around a large animal pen called a kraal,
and everyone would know everyone else.

We always have to wait for Daddy to get home so we can all eat together. If I were Masai, Daddy and Ray would be eating with the other men, and Mama and I with the other women.

Ray fills the water jug at the kitchen sink.
If I were Masai, my brother would walk
long distances to find a water hole, and he
would bring the water back in giant gourds.

"What's for pudding?" I ask.
Mama gives me money to buy a chocolate bar, and Ray
and I walk to the corner shop. If I were Masai and I wanted
something sweet, I would wait for the honey guide to come.
The little bird would chatter wildly above my head, begging me to
follow. I'd lope along below, and it would lead me to a beehive.
I'd light a fire with sticks rubbed hard together and make a smoking
torch to calm the bees. Then I would scoop the honeycomb and leave
enough behind for my friend the bird.

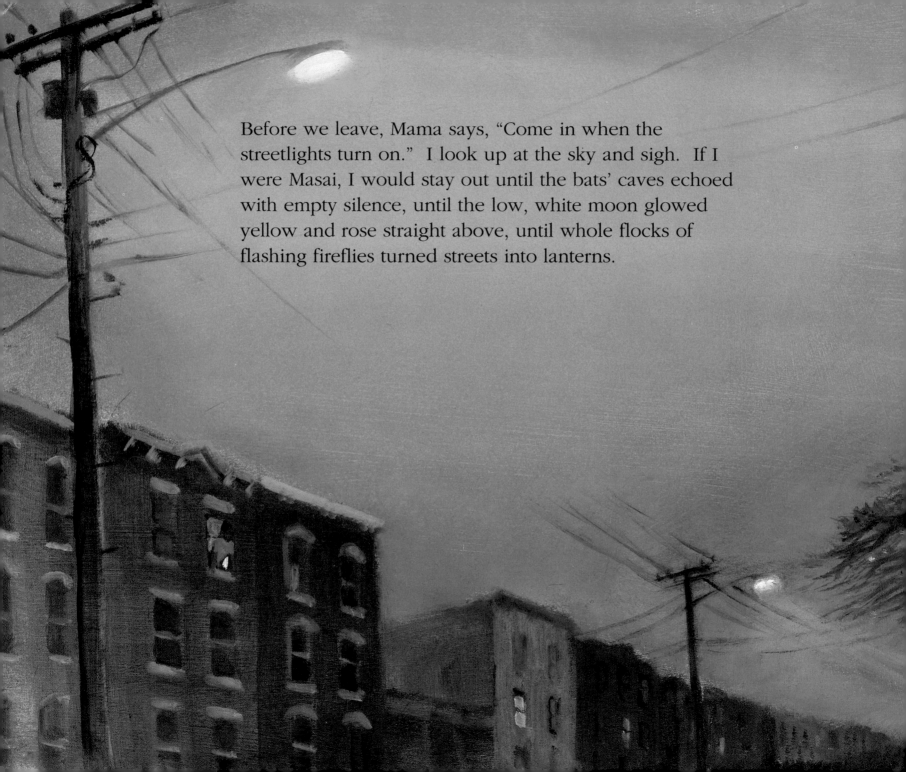

Before we leave, Mama says, "Come in when the streetlights turn on." I look up at the sky and sigh. If I were Masai, I would stay out until the bats' caves echoed with empty silence, until the low, white moon glowed yellow and rose straight above, until whole flocks of flashing fireflies turned streets into lanterns.

I would go inside then only to
sleep. I would not climb any stairs
if I were Masai. I would lift a
cowhide flap, and I'd be home.

If I were Masai, I couldn't look out of my window to see what's going on in the street below. My hut would have no windows, only small holes to let out smoke. We would not have couches, chairs, lamps, or tables, either – only several stools.

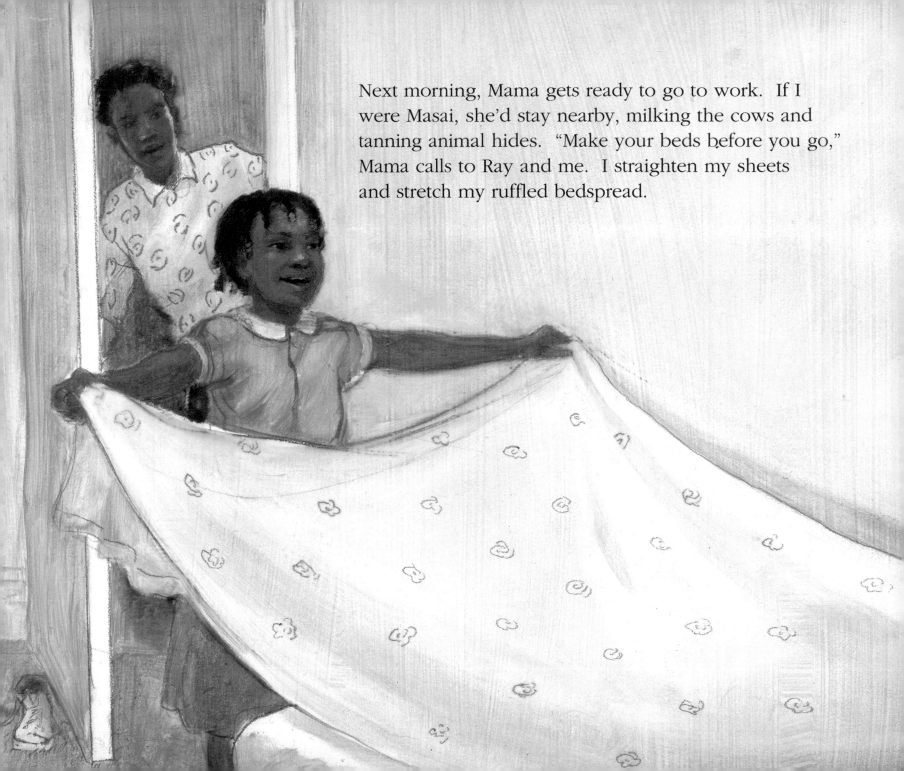

Next morning, Mama gets ready to go to work. If I were Masai, she'd stay nearby, milking the cows and tanning animal hides. "Make your beds before you go," Mama calls to Ray and me. I straighten my sheets and stretch my ruffled bedspread.

If I were Masai, I'd spread a cowhide on the bare earth floor at night and roll it back up in the morning.

I would not have my hamster, Huey, in his cage, if I were Masai. I would have cows, though, a whole herd, and I'd know every one by name!

I would not have to go to the zoo to see giraffes or ostriches, or zebras, either. I'd share the African air with them, the African soil, and the African rain.

I set out for school and run back in for my new white trainers.
I almost forgot – I have gym today. If I were Masai, I'd run
and leap in bare brown feet across lush pastures, or pale,
parched earth. And only once in a great, great while, I'd
wear sandals made of buffalo hide.

That evening, my brother and I fight over who gets the bathroom first. We're going to Grandma's party at a restaurant. It's her seventieth birthday. I wash with scented soap and dry my skin with a thick towel. If I were Masai preparing for a celebration, I'd rub my skin with cows' fat mixed with red clay so that my skin would shine. I'd want to smell nice if I were Masai, just like I do now, so I'd crush sweet-smelling leaves to rub along my shiny skin.

My cousin James comes over, and we pile into the car to drive to the party. If I were Masai, walking three miles would be nothing for me. I'd glide across grasslands, open and free.

Later, when her birthday dinner is over, Grandma
stares at me. "My, my, Linda," she says, "how slender
and graceful you are. Such a beautiful young girl!"
I kiss her with love and respect, just as I would if I
were Masai. If I were Masai, my name might be Eshe or
Hawa or Neema - or even Linde, almost like it is now.

I come home and stare at my reflection in my bedroom
mirror... smooth brown skin over high cheekbones and
black eyes that slant up a little when I smile. I like what I
see. I tingle again with that feeling about kinship.
I would look just like this if I were Masai.